The Goose with Noodles for Wings

Goodwin's story is dedicated to
children with Hypotonia and their families

The mama goose watched as Goodwin tried and failed to fly.

"I wish I could do it for him," she thought.

You see, Goodwin was a mighty fine goose.

But, he was just a wee bit different.

Goodwin could not fly.

Yet.

And as   Goodwin   stood there all by himself, he thought, "even the wind wants me to fly!"

You see,

everyone

can experience the wind, even with feet firmly planted on the ground.

Goodwin wanted to be like the other geese, to feel the effects of the wind.

So he would spread his wings and watch in amazement as his feathers ruffled in the breeze. Then he would lift his beak to the sky and giggle when a blast of air tickled his cheeks as his friends rushed by.

To get a wee bit stronger, Goodwin would climb up and down the big hill.

You see, Goodwin's legs were not like his friends'. They wobbled with each step he took and grew tired so quickly.

To make his noodle wings just a wee bit tougher, Goodwin would flap them up and down

You see, Goodwin's wings were not like his friends'. His wings were floppy, just like wet noodles. And it took all his energy to keep them straight.

She would gently fly him down to the
bottom of the big hill

to try again, and as she did Goodwin would tell himself,

"Someday, I will fly."

Day
    after
        day,

rain or shine, Goodwin could be seen struggling up the big hill and stopping at the top to spread his wings.

And then, with the wind at his back,
Goodwin would work his way down the hill,

hug his mama,

and do it all over a g a i n.

Until one day the top of the big hill was empty.

But where was Goodwin?

On this special day, Goodwin
climbed the hill as he always did,
spread his wings as he always did,
and lifted his beak as he always did.
But this day Goodwin was **different**, and the wind
seemed different too.

Goodwin's legs were now **stronger** from all those trips up and down the hill, his wings were now **tougher** from all of the flapping up and down,

and the wind, even though forceful,
welcomed Goodwin in mighty swirls above his head
as if saying,

"You can do it!"

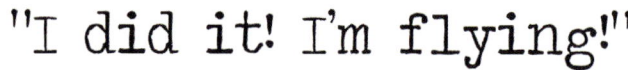

"I did it! I'm flying!"
Goodwin cried down to his mama
who was still waiting for him
at the bottom of the big hill.

His mama looked to the sky
and as she watched her son with complete admiration
she whispered, "I always knew you could,"
into a passing breeze.

About the Illustrator

Troy Goins of Athens, Ohio has been an artist for 10 years. He is an artist with autism who speaks about his personal experiences working in a local art studio and how it influenced him. Through his struggles he rose to his success in the field of art. He says, "a person is usually defined by what they can do, but when others judge them by their disability, their potential gets overshadowed." Troy strives to spread his idea of a better world for those with disabilities through the power of the arts.

Passion Works Studio is a collaborative community arts center located in Athens, Ohio at the foothills of the Appalachian Mountains. At the heart and soul of Passion Works is a core group of working artists with developmental differences. This collective creates aesthetically and conceptually powerful works of art. More important than what is produced, is how the collaborative practice encourages connection, purpose, and belonging for the individual artists and the community at large.

The Hypotonia Foundation would love to give special thanks to:

The Adkisson Family
Ivan and Mary Amato
Max Amato
Simon Amato
Brian Forsberg
Gregg and Denise Forsberg
Jake Forsberg
Ron and Suzanne Forsberg
The Gernandt Family
Troy Goins
The Hanson Family
Jane Hayden
Patricia Lovell
The Mariscal Family
Paula McKay
Ashton Morgan
Jim and Nancy Schade
Brittani Suazo

AFOBaby
Cascade DAFO
Huna Wristbands
Kozie Clothes
Passion Works Studio
Renuvee
Sawyer
TalkTools

Printed in Great Britain
by Amazon